Because I love
you I share
the excitement
of this book
with you —
Carol
1979

Arnie,
Knight of the Day

Also by

Donald Arneson

Doing Something Nice, Inc.
and Other Short Plays for Kids

Arnie, Knight of the Day

Written by

Donald Arneson

Illustrated by

Carol Schneider

BOOKMAKER PUBLISHING • BURNSVILLE

Library of Congress Cataloging in Publication Data

Arneson, Donald, 1932 —
    Arnie, Knight of the Day.

    SUMMARY: Presents six episodes in the life
of a 12-year-old living in a large city with his
divorced mother.
    (1. City and town life—Fiction. 2. Mother
and sons—Fiction) I. Schneider, Carol, 1938
— II. Title.
PZ7.A73398Ar (Fic) 79-18491

ISBN: 0-934778-01-9

To my mother and my J's

A special thanks to the students of Mrs. Cosgrove's 1978-79 sixth grade class at Gideon Pond Elementary School, Burnsville.

A special thanks to Ms. Becky Merrill.

CONTENTS

Chapter One

Arnie

"No one stays twelve forever, Arnie," Arnie's mother said to him. She said this in answer to his scowl. He had just asked her if he could go to the movies by himself that evening. However, not wanting him to walk alone through some of the worst area of the city, she had said no. Then he complained of being twelve, never having a chance to do "anything-ever!" and how badly she treated twelve-year-olds.

"I don't want you out alone in this rotten neighborhood," she argued.

They lived a few blocks off Franklin

Avenue in a three-story brick apartment building, a mile or so from downtown. The neighborhood was one of mid-sized apartment buildings, old houses converted into apartments, small stores and repair shops and few parks. It was mostly crowded and neglected, an area that had seen better times. Many of the people were drifters and Arnie's mother didn't trust some of the characters she saw on the streets.

Arnie insisted that his friend, Charlie Wainwright, was going too.

"I don't care. You're not," his mother insisted.

Arnie whined, "I never have any fun!"

His mother raised her voice to match his. "Oh, you poor boy! Your mother beats you every day, starves you, never buys you any clothes and, on top of that, she only lets you see one movie a week. It must be miserable!"

Arnie turned his head. He had been testing her and when she responded, as she usually did, by gently poking fun, it could make him break-up. If she saw his expression, it would have spoiled everything. He wanted her to think he was hurt.

She knew better. "Poor abused twelve-year-old," she said and wrapped her arms around him. He started giggling. "Guess you'll just have to stay home and watch color TV."

"There's nothing on."

She began tickling him. "Then go to bed," she said. In a second he was howling with laughter and trying desperately to escape.

"C'mon, Mom! Stop it!" he screamed between peels of laughter.

Finally she let him up, but he lay on the couch, panting.

"That isn't fair," he said. "You're too big."

"Hey, you! That isn't nice to say," she protested.

"Well, you can't help it if you're fat," he joked.

Of course, his mother was far from fat. Actually she was rather small, only slightly over five feet and not much more than a hundred pounds. She had long blonde hair, which always appeared freshly brushed. Her features were fine, her green eyes bright, alive. She was young and full of energy.

Arnie was almost his mother's height, but weighed no more than ninety-five. He was, as she said, "skin and bones". His hair, too, was blonde and his features fine, delicate like the white porcelain figurines one sees in gift shops. Though his brown eyes sparkled like his mother's, they were usually more serious and sometimes Arnie looked sad-faced.

Their apartment was on the third floor. It contained two bedrooms, a living room, bath, kitchen and small eating area. It had the room they wanted. If they had moved to a nicer neighborhood, they would have had to pay twice as much for the same thing. So they put up with the narrow crowded streets, the old unpainted houses, the drifters and seedy looking characters who roamed the streets.

Since his mother and father had separated, his mother had been working as a secretary for a trucking firm. His father had moved to another part of the city. At first his father had visited Arnie regularly, but after a while the visits had dropped off and now he didn't come very often. Before the separation they had lived farther out, but that had been when Arnie was younger. Actually it was hard to remember anything else but living alone with his mother and seeing his father on rare occasions and since that was the way it was, it seemed okay.

About a mile away on the bus line Arnie's grandfather lived in a small apartment and Arnie would take the bus there by himself on Saturdays. That was kind of fun—going off by himself like that. And usually his grandfather had some treat for him. If nothing else, he would slip Arnie a dollar to spend for anything he liked.

Years ago his grandfather had been a farmer, but now he lived by himself and didn't do much but grow flowers in a window box and play cards with his buddies. Arnie had seen pictures of the farm, faded black and white pictures of a lot of people he couldn't remember—uncles and aunts and cousins and so forth, one of his grandmother, who had died before he was born, interesting pictures of threshing machines, horses pulling hayracks, family outings, parties,

MY MOM   GOP

MY UNCLE   ME

MY ALBUM
ARNIE

weddings, things like that. The one that really got to him, however, was one of his mother as a little girl riding on his grandfather's shoulders. It looked so funny seeing his own mother like that! It was hard to imagine the person he knew as his mother being the little girl in the picture. People could really change!

Often his grandfather talked about change, mostly how his own life had changed. Once he had been a farmer making his living off the land. Though it had been hard work and sometimes miserable, it had been "a good life". Then that had all changed. For some reason the bank took the farm and he was forced to move to the city to work. That had been many years ago. Arnie had heard the story many times.

As his grandfather said, "We just pulled up stakes and moved to the city, the whole kit and caboodle." That meant grandfather, grandmother, Arnie's mother, who was a young girl then, and her older brother, Arnie's uncle. Grandfather had gotten a job in a factory. He worked with his hands as always, only now it was the same task over and over and he couldn't be outside and be his own boss, make his own plans, harvest his own grain. Grandmother had died, Arnie's mother grew up and married, his uncle grew up, went to work and moved into a hotel apartment. Soon grandfather retired and took a little one room apartment. Things had changed a lot.

Though it made him sad, Arnie's grandfather liked to talk about all these changes. At least, he liked to get out the old black photo album and show the pictures to Arnie, pointing to this person and that, telling little stories about them.

Arnie enjoyed stories of how his mother and uncle behaved when they were children. One he especially liked was how his uncle at six or seven splattered two dozen fresh eggs against the barn door, pitching each one like a baseball and how grandfather hauled him off to the grove, pulled down his pants and spanked his bare behind. It was funny— hard to imagine his uncle doing it—but really funny.

Arnie was very fond of his uncle. He loved his easy-going, relaxed manner. More than anything, though, he loved his comical face. Arnie could never decide whether his uncle was ugly or handsome. His nose was crooked like a prize fighter's, his chin jutted out too far and his face seemed sort of lopsided. But it was a fun face, always smiling a silly smile.

Though he was not big, Arnie's uncle was very strong. His muscles bulged through his shirts, his body was trim and hard. He was like a gymnast, not too tall or heavy, but quite muscular. He worked as a construction laborer, usually operating the heavy equipment. He lived in one room in a hotel, but visited Arnie and his mother a lot, eating most of his meals with them.

Arnie's bedroom was small but exceptionally neat considering it was filled with furniture and things that were so important to him. One wall was plastered with posters, every inch of space covered with the bright printing and colorful pictures: rock stars, skiers, animals, mountains, valleys, winter scenes, summer scenes, some with clever sayings. A bright, psychedelic wall. Besides the bed and dresser the room contained two desks and chairs and a card table. Upon these were placed works in progress, such as: a castle which he was building out of brightly colored stones, a collection of maps, a collection of small plastic cars, a collection of clay animals, a few stuffed animals—relics of an earlier age—weapons, rockets, odds and ends. On one small corner of one of the desks was space for school books, at the moment vacant. Everything was in its place, neat and ordered, well-arranged.

To escape his mother Arnie ran from the living room to his bedroom. She chased him. He tried to keep her out, but she placed her shoulder to the door before he could close it. A struggle ensued, each pushing against the door. Arnie was still laughing.

"C'mon, Mom!" he pleaded. He was growing weak.

"You called me fat, you little rat! I'm going to get you."

"Mom!"

Finally he gave up and slid to the floor. She practically tumbled into his room and fell on top of him.

"Mom, don't tickle me anymore," he muttered, nearly out of breath.

"Okay." As she held him down, she considered her next move. "Am I fat?" she asked.

"No."

"Okay!"

She let him up. Exhausted, he fell on his bed.

"Arnie, how can you keep your room so neat?"

He shrugged. Actually it was easy since he liked to have everything in order.

"Boys your age are supposed to live in awful messes."

"Just because you - - - - - -," he began, then caught himself. It was going to be another joke for which she would tickle him. She was not messy, but then she was not as neat as he. "I didn't mean it! I didn't mean it!" he protested.

She laughed. "It always amazes me. Your room is spotless. You sure don't take after your mother in that respect."

"Grandpa," he said. "Grandpa's neat."

"Yes. When are you going to see him?"

"Oh . . . . . maybe next Saturday. One of these days we're going to take a train

11

trip up north to Duluth.''

"You and your grandfather are good buddies, aren't you!"

"Yeah. We do lots of fun things together.''

"You do fun things with Hal.''

"Yeah. He's neat too.''

His uncle Hal took him to baseball games and fishing sometimes; also he played ball with him and wrestled and did other fun things like go to the movies. Hal was really neat.

"Well, listen kid,'' she said, half serious. "I want you to stay home and behave.''

"Where are you going?'' he asked.

"Out.''

"I gotta stay home alone?''

"You'll be all right. Don't cry.''

"It's not that - - - - - - -.''

"Well, I don't want you going to the movies because when I go out I want to know that you're home. And you can stay home by yourself because I don't make you do it that much. And you can watch TV or work on one of your collections or something. Maybe you can mess up your room for a change.'' Her mouth twisted into a tiny smile.

"Very funny," he declared.

After she left, Arnie raised the window in his room. Though it was spring, the night air was chilly. He swung the screen out, lifted it off its hinges and pulled it inside the room. He sat on the window ledge with his feet still inside the room. He leaned far out by hanging onto the window frame. The sky seemed a silky, shimmering black, the stars small cut-outs laid on this background. He inhaled the delicious crisp air.

He thought how unhappy his mother would be if she knew what he was doing. There would be no kidding about this!

Five feet below Arnie's window was the slanting roof of the adjoining building, a business establishment. He slipped backward out the window and, clutching the ledge, lowered himself down the wall to the roof. Then he simply followed the slope upward to the front of the building. There he had placed a wooden box. By standing on the box he could reach the top of his apartment building. Digging his toes into the crevices between the bricks, he scaled the wall and reached the roof. From there he had a view of the city skyline.

Sitting with his back against the short brick wall that rimmed the roof of the building, Arnie would watch the city and dream. And above all Arnie was a dreamer! When he looked above the trees at the towering structures of the city, now all asparkle, he saw castles, space ships, magic cities, magic mountains, the past, the future, dreams, hopes, desires and adventures galore.

Directly in front of him the city's tallest building appeared to split the sky in two. Squares of lights here and there decorated the side of the building. He tried to imagine what it was like to stand at the top and look out at the city below. What a fantastic sight it must be! He thought of the astronauts looking down at the earth from the moon. He thought of himself on a space craft far beyond the earth and moon, looking back, looking ahead at Saturn, Jupiter, the galaxies, moving out, out.

Before long he realized that he had been dozing. Holy Cats! He couldn't let his mother catch him out here! No more time for dreaming. He scrambled back to the roof of the next building, dropping with a thud and scurried back to his window. Here he reached up for the window ledge and, like a squirrel, scampered up the wall and fell into the room. He replaced the screen and closed the window.

When he looked at the clock, he saw that it wasn't as late as he thought. What a relief! As pleasant as his mother usually was, he didn't think she would appreciate his journeys to the roof. Undressing quickly, he turned out the light and climbed into bed. When he closed his eyes, he could still see the bright skyline. He settled back pleasantly to dream some more. He loved to dream.

Chapter Two

Ninnyhammer

Arnie sat in his look-out at the end of the alley that bordered the freeway. At the moment he looked like a huge moth because he was encased in a mass of blankets, quilts and old rags—part of his disguise. His look-out was a packing crate upon which he had erected a cardboard castle. He peered with eager eyes at the tall craggy buildings of the city that rose up from the other side of the criss-cross of entrance and exit ramps.

Arnie saw the city as an ancient castle with turrets, catwalks and flying banners. And he was a spy watching for knights to charge across the drawbridge to attack his position. Then he would be ready to ride to meet them. He would shed his disguise, don his battle dress, leap onto his horse and dash off to the war.

Sound the alarm! Sound the trumpets! Attack! He saw it all: horses charging abreast, knights with lances drawn, the opposing lines tangling in a mass of confusion. Out of it he rode victorious.

With some difficulty Arnie stood and then slowly squirmed out of his cocoon. With his disguise at his feet he turned his attention to other things. Baseball. It was time to head for the stadium. In a vacant lot next to the alley he had made a simple pitcher's mound. Springing from the look-out, he scooped up his ball and glove and strolled to the mound.

The game was to throw the rubberized baseball against the side of one of the sheds that lined the alley. Already the shed showed signs of wear from his fastball. But Arnie had all the pitches: slider, sinker, change-of-pace. He loved to hear the roar of the crowd as he pitched in the World Series.

Leaning forward, he took the sign from

his catcher, went into the wind-up and delivered a fastball. Strike! Next he served up a slider. Strike two! The first two batters went down by strike-outs; the last one popped up. He went through the batting order with no trouble. In the fourth, one man got a scratch single, but was erased by a double play. His side scored only one run, but it seemed to be enough; he was mowing them down right and left.

In the bottom of the ninth the other team put two men on with two outs. The last batter ran the count to three-two. The last pitch! Arnie checked the runners and delivered. The ball shot past him and down the alley. He took off and chased it as it avoided the obstacles in the alley, scooped it up before it entered the busy street and faked a perfect side-arm throw to first base.

The game was over! They had won the Series! The winning pitcher was mobbed by fans and players as he made his way to the dug-out and the showers.

Arnie walked along the sidewalk. When he came to the intersection, he stopped, stooped over and, in quarterback fashion, called the signal for a real razzle-dazzle play. Then he hunched forward, set for the snap. "Hut! Hut!" he barked. With the snap of the ball, he took one step to the side and then ran forward, weaving his way downfield, side-stepping one tackler after another.

* * *

This same Saturday morning was like any morning for Ninnyhammer. He lay as usual with his paws folded in front of him, one eye partly open, listening for the movement of his master. Ninnyhammer was part Lab, other parts unknown.

The little apartment in which he lived, not far from Arnie's, was musty. The one lone window rattled from the slightest gust of wind and the light that entered was faint. When Ninnyhammer's master finally arose from his chair by the window, Ninnyhammer sprang to his feet.

Slowly his master, a fragile, little old man, shuffled across the room and let out his dog as he did every morning at this time.

Outside Ninnyhammer sniffed the air. His ears adjusted to the loud city noises.

Down the street he saw mammoth yellow monsters sprawled out, pawing and gulping huge bites out of the street, making a terrible racket. Disgusted, he turned and ran in the opposite direction.

He loved to trot along, gliding effortlessly, his head swinging carelessly from side to side. He loved the chance to be free, if only for a little while. Once he paused to watch some children playing, but resisted the idea of joining them. He decided to just wander.

* * *

Meanwhile, after a long run, first as a football player, then a track star and finally an Indian scout, Arnie staggered onto the freeway bridge near his house. From the bridge he could watch the cars slip by beneath him, dashing to and from the city. The castle.

Here Arnie's sport was pretending to dump caldrons of boiling oil on the knights who passed underneath, just like the defenders on the castle walls. Or he would bomb the cars—spit bomb them. Then he calculated their speed very accurately, put his mouth up to the mesh fence on the bridge and let go of the bomb at just the right split second. It was great fun watching the bombs sail down on the traffic.

* * *

When Ninnyhammer reached the freeway near the same bridge, he saw an unusual sight. He saw this stranger, a boy involved in wild antics, jumping up and down and pressing his mouth to the wire fence. Very odd!

He stood behind the freeway fence and barked at the boy. "Hey, boy! What are you doing?" he seemed to say.

However, because of the traffic noise, Arnie did not hear and after a short while he walked away to the other side of the freeway. Then, when Arnie was directly opposite Ninnyhammer, he happened to turn. Spotting the dog, he cupped his hands to his mouth and called. Then he scaled the fence, called again, whistled and waved. Actually he was just being silly, but, nevertheless, Ninnyhammer became excited and whined and pawed at the ground.

Then he ran up and down, looking for

a way over the fence. He tried jumping, but the fence was too high and had sharp points on the top. When Arnie started walking away, Ninnyhammer kept pace with him and soon found a ramp that led down to the freeway.

Here the cars, flashing by in their slots, frightened him. In spite of that he started toward Arnie, who stood behind the fence across the freeway far above him.

Arnie was really astonished to see the dog down on the freeway and equally amazed at how insignificant he appeared, almost like a tiny toy. And when the animal moved toward him and all that traffic, he shouted, "No! No! Get back!" Crazy dog, he thought. What's he up to?

Ninnyhammer approached the first lane of traffic timidly, then leaped onto the pavement, moving unsteadily as if treading on ice. Cars swerved to avoid him. From Arnie's viewpoint the traffic seemed to swallow him. It was as if the dog had entered a lion's den.

Lowering his head, Arnie held his breath and closed his eyes. When he looked up, he saw that somehow the dog had reached the median strip. Determined to rescue it, Arnie started down a nearby freeway ramp. As he descended, he waved his arms, motioning Ninny-hammer to go back.

At the bottom of the ramp Arnie turned and headed toward the dog, who stood nervously on a little island of grass. Now only one pavement, like a narrow but treacherous stream, separated them.

Because the dog looked so helpless, Arnie tried, above the noise, to reassure him. "Take it easy, boy. I'll help you," he shouted. But then, before he could do anything, Ninnyhammer leaped again into the storm of angry, screaming cars. He was caught in mid-air, tossed upward and nose-dived in a heap back on the median. There he lay perfectly still except for the slight movement of his fur as it was struck by the wind.

In that instant of impact Arnie slumped forward as though punched in the stomach. He squeezed his eyes shut. For several moments he remained frozen in that position, hoping that when he did open his eyes, he would see the friendly dog standing there wagging his tail. Only he didn't.

If only I hadn't waved! Arnie thought regretfully. If only I hadn't pretended he was a wild animal and whistled at him! If only!

Rising unsteadily, Arnie waited for the traffic, then darted over to the body. He touched it gently, then adjusted Ninny-hammer's head, which had been twisted awkwardly to one side.

He looks like he's asleep, mused Arnie. But he had heard about the deceitfulness of death.

The sight of Ninnyhammer's legs evoked a picture of a hunting dog running through fields of grass.

Arnie felt the dog's neck for a collar, but there was none. "I wonder what your name is," Arnie said. "And who you belong to. Well, I guess I'll have to pretend you were mine. I'll just have to do what has to be done!" he exclaimed, rising and glaring angrily at the traffic.

As soon as he could, he crossed to the ramp and scrambled back to the streets. He went directly to the dilapidated shed that he used for pitch-ball and began sorting through the old tools and building materials he had seen stored there. He broke a red slat from a snow fence in two, formed the pieces into a cross and bound them with string he found on the floor. With a yellow carpenter's crayon he wrote on the slat, "Here lies dog."

Next he scrounged around for the other items he needed: a vase—actually an old peanut butter jar—and a spade. Then he began the trek back.

Back on the street he became sort of apprehensive because he wondered if he might be attracting too much attention and he didn't know what to expect from the adults he met. Maybe they would stop him and ask questions and keep him from doing what had to be done. However, they ignored him and soon he reached the bridge.

There, along the fence he went in search of flowers. Since the idea of flowers along the freeway seemed strange, he really didn't expect to find any. He was surprised, therefore, when he found a few tiny wild violets hiding in the grass.

Now, with the flowers in the vase, he was ready. Yet he hesitated. It occurred to him that since the dog was not his, he did not have to do this. He could just walk away. Sooner or later someone would pick up the body.

No! The dog deserved more than that. Besides, he had been responsible. No! He would do his duty.

He went back down the ramp. At the edge of the freeway he paused a moment to look up at the city. The cars were like knights charging out to drive him away. But he was not afraid of them! No! He would stand his ground. The sound of trumpets stirred him. He raised his lance, ready for the onslaught.

At the next break in the traffic he hurried over to Ninnyhammer. "All right, boy, I'll take care of you now," he declared, standing over the dog.

Where he began to dig the ground was hard and gravelly and he ran into pieces of concrete. But he was determined! He wanted to make this the dog's final resting place. The dog was a soldier and this was the field of battle.

When Arnie had ripped out what he hoped was the last shovelful of earth, he threw down the shovel and measured the

hole. Then he stood erect and began the ceremony.

"I didn't know him," he said, "but I'm sure he was a good dog."

After a few more words, he gently lowered the limp body into the grave, scooped up some dirt and solemnly intoned, "Ashes to ashes, dust to dust," something he had heard in a movie. He sprinkled the dirt over Ninnyhammer.

After he had filled in the grave, he planted the cross into the loose earth and set the jar of violets on the mound. Then he saluted. He had done his duty!

As Arnie reached for the shovel, he noticed a couple of interested faces turned his way, two boys in the back of a station wagon that was just speeding by. He watched them as they pressed their faces to the glass. Finally he waved and they waved back. Then he hoisted the shovel to his shoulder, slipped back through the traffic and hiked up the ramp.

Chapter Three

Gop

Gop, as Arnie called his grandfather, leaned out of the window of his apartment, which was located in a rather run-down area of the city, and watched Arnie playing three floors below. He was both happy and sad.

It was a beautiful, warm, spring day, but there was practically no view, unless you could call the brick wall of the opposing building a few feet away a view. So often on days like this Gop yearned for a better sight. He wanted to see the countryside. Unfortunately he was surrounded by a dreary forest of buildings that all but blocked out the sky.

In the flower box his begonias were struggling for life. Gop was annoyed to see them always covered with soot from the city smog.

"Brave begonias," he declared, blowing off the soot and dust.

"Hey, Gop!" Arnie shouted from below. Then Gop realized he had been daydreaming, not watching his grandson as expected. Arnie wanted to throw a ball up to him. He cocked his arm.

"No, Arnie, you might break a window," Gop warned.

What a shame! Gop thought. The boy doesn't know what it's like to see the country or smell good clean air.

Withdrawing from the window, Gop returned to his morning coffee. His apartment was very small, only one room with a tiny kitchenette in one corner. It, too, made him sad. It was like a prison cell. Yet there was no other place for him. He was an old man with no place to go. On an impulse he crossed to a mirror on the wall and peered at himself.

Yes, he said to himself, I look as old as I am. Seventy-five. Even older. Maybe eighty-five.

Yet the face he saw was not heavily lined. It was round and full. The hair was thin and white, but he was not entirely bald. The eyes were still lively. Most people would have called him nice-looking; of course, he did not see himself as others did, at least, not today.

"You're a crazy, stupid old man!" he blared at his image. "What are you doing living in this hole?"

What can I do? he asked himself. Nothing. Absolutely nothing.

Back at the table he soon lost himself in his thoughts, that is, until Arnie burst into the room.

"Goodness! What's the rush?" Gop asked.

Arnie held onto the table, panting. "I just came up to see what you were doing."

"I'm getting ready to run away from home," Gop declared. "I'm fed up with this place. I'm leaving. Just running away."

Arnie did not know what to say. Old men didn't run away, he knew. Just kids.

"I'm running away! Right now!" Gop proclaimed with sudden energy and rose and nearly leaped to the dresser where he began pulling clothes out of the drawer. "What are you supposed to take with you when you run away?" he asked, and then turned and dashed into the bathroom. "Toothbrush and toothpaste for one thing. Let's see . . . deodorant. No reason you can't smell good even if you are running away. Gotta travel light though."

On his way back to the dresser he rummaged through the closet and pulled out an old canvas zipper bag. His face was flushed and he seemed full of life.

"Gee, Arnie," he said, "running away from home can be fun!"

"Are you really?" Arnie asked. All along he had thought Gop had been kidding.

"Sure. Why can't old men run away? Kids do it all the time."

Gop stuffed his things into the bag and then zipped it shut. After a moment's thought he opened it, went to the refrigerator and got some food for a snack. Now he could scarcely close the bag.

Realizing that Gop was serious, Arnie asked if he could go along. "You have school," Gop answered. "Besides, your mother wouldn't like it."

"She wouldn't like it if she knew you were running away, either," Arnie responded.

Gop smiled. "Okay, you can go part way."

They went to a nearby park where they often spent some time on Arnie's visits. This was also where Gop would pass the day with his old friends, other bachelors and widowers who lived in retirement in the neighborhood.

In a distant corner of the park a number of Gop's friends sat playing pinochle. As Gop and Arnie arrived, one of the players moved over on his bench and asked Gop to join them.

"No. Don't have time," Gop said. "I'm running away from home."

Those within earshot laughed. Running away? Who ever heard of such a thing?

"What's so strange about that?" Gop demanded. "I'm sick of the city and this life so I'm going to leave. Just decided

35

a little while ago. Just like that." And he snapped his fingers for emphasis.

However, he could see they still didn't take him seriously. No one did. Arnie, who had been climbing a tree, came and stood beside his grandfather. "He doesn't believe me either. My own grandson!" Gop said. At that moment the sound of semi-trucks on the highway practically drowned out his voice.

As Gop and Arnie left, a few of the old men called, "Don't run too far!" And, "Write if you get work." It was just a big joke to them. Most of them, however, hadn't even looked up from their game.

"They don't understand how I feel," Gop complained. "Maybe they think old men shouldn't have feelings. I can just hear them saying, 'Why doesn't he act his age?' People expect us to sit around doing nothing but twiddle our thumbs."

At the first street light Gop turned to Arnie and asked, "How do you get out of this town?"

Arnie shrugged. He had never been out of the city. Gop shook his head sadly. Already he was lost.

They passed through the neighborhood of run-down apartment buildings and arrived at the freeway, but the heavy traffic bothered Gop. There was a foot bridge that crossed over the freeway, but he refused to go on it. So they turned and walked north toward downtown. It was pleasant. On the way they met some little girls playing with a puppy and Gop stopped to talk to them. One of the girls grabbed Gop around the leg and he lifted her up and hugged her.

A block farther on they encountered a man planting flowers by his front steps and stopped again to talk. Gop introduced Arnie as his partner and said they were on an African safari. They all laughed. Gop had known the man slightly, but had never really talked to him. They talked about flowers and the problem of raising them in the city.

After they resumed their walk, Gop told Arnie that he thought he would just travel around the country hitching rides or catching a bus, riding the rails, fishing in mountain streams, sleeping out under the stars, doing whatever struck his fancy. In other words: being a vagabond.

To Arnie it all sounded really super.

Finally they came to a tree-lined mall in the heart of the city and as they walked along admiring its beauty, they almost tripped over a girl sitting on the sidewalk. She had a guitar on her lap and she was enjoying the sun. Gop was a little shocked by her clothes, which consisted of bib-overalls and flannel shirt, but she was friendly and they started talking and she began asking questions.

When she found out that Gop was running away from home, she didn't laugh at all. Instead she composed a song in Gop's honor and played it for Gop and Arnie and any passers-by who cared to stop and listen.

She sang: "Going on a trip today,
A long trip;
Running away.
Going to be a wanderer,
Going a long, long, long
way."

Gop was flattered. They said good-by to the girl. They could hear her still playing a block away.

"Well, Arnie," Gop commented, "that was a nice send-off."

They continued north. The street was bustling with noon hour activity. People were out for lunch and, since it was such a nice spring day, some people ate on the curb or the benches along the mall.

When they reached the end of the mall, they turned and walked east two blocks to a bus stop.

"We can catch a bus to the edge of town," Gop said. "Of course, you gotta go home later," he added quickly.

In the bus across the aisle from Gop and Arnie sat an elderly woman and a young girl. When Gop and the woman looked at each other, they both smiled. Gop commented on the weather and then they chatted for a little while. It became a pleasant ride. At the end of the line they exited together, but went separate ways.

Gop and Arnie strolled down to a lake a block away from the city bus line. They were now on the edge of the city, but more in the country than the city. They stopped to watch the sail boats and motor boats. Gop was enjoying the sights, pausing frequently to admire the sail

boats. He would take a deep breath and remark, "Oh, this is really great, Arnie!"

Arnie was happy that his grandfather was finally happy because it seemed that so much of the time lately he had been sad and sort of down in the dumps. They just walked along the beach, watching the boats and Arnie skipped stones on the water. Then after a while they stopped and had a snack from the things Gop had packed.

After an hour or so they hiked back to the highway. Gop was a little nervous. This was the highway he would follow as he began his life as a run-away. He looked down the road, thinking of where it could lead him. Actually it could lead him anywhere—anywhere at all. There was nothing to stop him. He was a grown-up; he could do whatever he liked with his life.

Soon he turned to look in the other direction, back toward the city. Should he return to it? In many ways it was like a prison and yet . . . . .

"Should I go, Arnie?" he asked. But Arnie did not answer, since Gop answered for him: "I think what I'm going to do is . . . . . . run away . . . . . . but just for little trips, like today . . . . . . and whenever I go again, I'll take you with me. And sometimes we'll go for longer journeys. We'll explore together—you and me. We'll be vagabonds together. Whenever your old grandfather has to get away from the smelly old city, we'll run away, huh?"

"Gee that'd be great!" Arnie exclaimed. "Could we take a train ride some day? I've never been on a train."

"Sure. We'll do all kinds of fun things," Gop promised.

Back at the bus stop they met the woman and young girl. Gop was surprised to see them since he had assumed they lived out here in the suburbs.

The woman said, "I just come out here with my granddaughter once in a while, just to get away. Otherwise I would go crazy there in the city."

As Gop helped her up the steps, he said with a sympathetic nod, "Yeah, I know what you mean. I do the same thing."

Chapter Four

The Little Old Lady Who Lived in the Pits

Ever since that first day when he sat overlooking the abandoned gravel pit and the icy winds ran up crevices cut by the rain, Arnie kept seeing the old lady in his mind. It had been such an enormous pit it would have been easy to have missed the old lady's shack, which was buried in a distant corner. He found it because of the cats. At first he almost ran away, but then moved cautiously toward their yowling. There was a whole flock of them perched on broken crates and swarming around overturned pails. Behind them was the shack. Right in the

middle of a gravel pit!

Only when he looked closely could he see that someone was living in it. There were flowerboxes beneath the two small windows and a hint of curtains behind the black grimy panes. A trickle of dark smoke flowed from a metal pipe in the center of the roof.

After seeing the smoke he backed away, hid behind a washout and waited. He just felt he had to find out who lived in such a strange place. While he sat shaking from the cold, he imagined all sorts of strange creatures but not the squat old woman who finally appeared dressed all in black with a woolen scarf tied tightly around her head. She threw food to the cats, turned quickly and, scraping her feet along the ground, retreated back into the shack.

On his way home Arnie told himself he had made an important discovery and vowed he would keep going back until he had learned more about this strange creature.

When he got home, he found his uncle sitting on the outside steps of the apartment building where Arnie and his mother lived. His uncle was a very easy-going man with a funny looking face. His nose appeared broken, like a prize fighter's, though it really wasn't, just a little crooked. His mouth was usually twisted into a puzzling, friendly smile.

He was a heavy equipment operator; however, he was out of work a lot, especially in the winter. Then he often picked up Arnie and together they went different places, like to hockey games. Sometimes in the spring and summer they went to baseball games. In the fall they would watch football on T.V.

Tonight Arnie was surprised to see his uncle sitting there like that because it was so chilly. In fact, by the time he arrived home, there was some snow in the air— hard little chunks of snow-ice that stung Arnie's cheeks.

"Hey, what's the matter?" Arnie asked.

"I don't know. Something is, but I can't figure it out," his uncle replied.

"What do you mean?"

"There was something bothering me when I got up this morning and it's been eating at me all day."

"Well, what's it like?"

"Like something's gonna happen."

"That's funny."

"That's for sure. The first thing I thought about this morning was that snake and the little mouse. I don't know why. Can't figure it out to save me, but when I woke up, even before I got out of bed, it just struck me. You remember I told you about that?"

Yes, Arnie nodded, he remembered. Especially, he remembered the way his uncle told the story and how it bothered him. Anyway, his uncle had been in Redfield, South Dakota where he had been working on a road job—driving the big cats—and when he had some spare time one day while they were shut down waiting for it to dry from a rain they'd had the night before, he went off walking by himself. He came to a river and it was beautiful there, the water trickling over the rocks, making a lonely sound.

He crossed a small dam and went on up a hill to a cemetery and there he read the headstones, thinking how most of the people were forgotten now, the names just names. But it was peaceful and he wanted to escape the noise of the cat. While he sat enjoying the sights, he heard a faint squealing sound. He saw the grass move and when he moved over to it, he saw a snake with a tiny mouse way down its throat; only the mouse was still wriggling. It made him feel uneasy. After the mouse had disappeared, he walked away, but the impression stayed with him. It was life and death.

"Well, I keep seeing that snake and hearing that mouse," he insisted. "That's why I think it's a sign that something's gonna happen."

"Maybe," Arnie conceded. "But it's cold here."

"Your mother's not in," his uncle said.

"Where is she? She should be home by now."

"Maybe she missed the bus," his uncle suggested. "Or maybe she's shopping. Women always gotta go shopping. If they were in the middle of the Sahara Desert, they'd have to go shopping."

Arnie smiled and said, "Yeah." After a few moments of silence, Arnie ventured, "I saw an old lady today living down in an old gravel pit. You know that gravel pit by the freeway?''

''Yeah.''

''She was living in a gravel pit!'' Arnie had expected his news to really surprise his uncle. Instead, he only shook his head slowly and clicked his tongue against the roof of his mouth. ''Maybe that's a sign too,'' Arnie suggested. His uncle nodded. Arnie continued, ''She looked so sad. She's real old. I mean **real** old. I'll bet she's ninety or so and she's got the place full of cats!''

''What do you wanna do about it?'' his uncle asked.

''I don't know, but it bothered me. All she's got is those cats. Living there in a dirty old shack! Gosh! You couldn't even see through the windows.''

His uncle looked up at the sky that was spitting even more B-B size pieces of snow. ''You'll find some way to help her,'' he said. He opened his mouth and let the little chunks land on his tongue. Then after a few seconds: ''Will you help me when I'm old and lonely like that?''

''Sure, I will,'' Arnie answered.

His uncle said, ''Boy! I wish I could get that outta my mind, that thing about

the snake and the mouse. What d'ya
think that means?''

"I don't know.'' Arnie wrapped his arms
around himself.

"I just can't move,'' his uncle said, seeing Arnie was shivering. "I gotta stay
right here until I get that out of my mind.''
Then, after some thought, he added,
"That old lady, she's like the mouse. She
gets gobbled up.''

"By what?'' Arnie asked.

"By the city,'' his uncle answered. "So
do I. So do most of us. We're so small.
It just eats us alive.''

Finally Arnie squatted down at his
uncle's feet and turned his back to the
snow.

"I've been thinking about the country a
lot lately,'' his uncle admitted.

Arnie recalled the times his uncle talked about the farm on which he was raised.
In fact, he wanted to ask him to tell about
the times when he herded cattle. That
was when he was a boy Arnie's age. He
and a neighbor kid would graze the cattle
in a large area that had been leased from
the railroad. When the cattle were con-
tentedly grazing, there wasn't much to do

except keep them away from the tracks. Then he and his friend would play. Maybe they would swim in an old mud hole they called their swimming pool. Or they would ride the horse, Ol' Jim. The friend had practiced so he could fall off the horse without getting hurt so they worked out a game using that special talent. His uncle would crouch behind a clump of grass and be an ambushing Indian and the friend would gallop the horse at him. Using a singletree for a rifle, he would fire and the neighbor, shot, would clutch his heart, scream and fall off in a place where the earth was freshly plowed. When his uncle told Arnie about it, he said that it had looked so real he could hardly believe it was acting.

Arnie thought how great it would have been growing up on a farm and especially having a horse to ride and cattle to herd just like a real cowboy.

Finally his uncle said, "Why don't you go in? I'm staying outside until it's dark. Besides, I'm not staying for supper."

"Why not?"

"Oh, I dunno. I been stopping too much and it's a lot of work for your mother.''

"No it isn't. Why don't you stay?''

Without any warning his uncle sprang to his feet, grabbed Arnie by the back of the neck and faked a punch to the stomach and a jab to the chin. Then he smiled and barked, "Hey, what do you know about it, you bum? You don't have to cook. No. Your mother works real hard all day. Maybe I'll come over in a couple of days and take you both out for dinner. How about that?''

Arnie thought about what he could have at a restaurant and drooled.

"That would be great!''

However, it was more than a couple of days before Arnie saw his uncle again. In the meantime he made several visits back to the gravel pit. In those few days he had undergone a complete cycle of feelings toward the old woman. On the first day she had been only an odd sight. After his uncle had talked about the mouse and the snake, he had considered her loneliness.

One day he found her sitting by the front door stirring something in a big pot. It happened then that she looked up and he saw her face and it seemed twisted in an ugly scowl. After that he thought of witches.

At school he asked some of his friends about her. They didn't know much, but they were fascinated by the idea that she might be a witch. Somebody said they had heard she had committed a murder once and that she could cast a spell if one looked into her eyes. Some of his friends made plans to go to the pit to spy on her; however, Arnie worried about what they might do to her and talked them out of it. That was when he came full circle and started feeling sorry for her again.

He tried to imagine what it was like living in the shack. When he saw her carrying little bundles of sticks inside, he reasoned she had a wood stove. There were no electric lines running to the house. Occasionally she would throw out a bucket of water. But where did she get fresh water? Did she have a pump? Old ladies who kept cats usually had lots of plants too, but the windows were so sooted over it was hard to tell. And what did she do all day? How did she get food?

She became a mystery, a mystery that

walked in old clod-hopper shoes, a baggy, billowy dress and wrapped her head in a ragged scarf.

It was strange how she treated the cats—never petting or calling them, practically ignoring them, except that she did feed them regularly. When she came out with their food, they erupted like rats from under the shack, yowling, leaping over one another, springing along like one lively mass to the same spot each day. She would bring out a broom, whacking at them, and sweep the dirt in the spot. Then she would hurry back to the house and return with a pan or an apron drooping with scraps.

Arnie went for nearly two weeks without seeing his uncle and missed him very much, especially on Sundays when they used to do so many things together. They might take a bus to Minnehaha Creek and walk along the banks. That was nice. It was like being in the country. They would walk along and his uncle would flush the dead leaves up with a kick of his foot. Under the huge trees it was quiet and peaceful and the ground felt soft and pliable.

One day his uncle showed up in the apartment looking very tired, his face covered with a scraggly beard. His eyes were red-rimmed. Arnie had come home from school and found him sitting at the kitchen table.

"Hi, Arnie," he said, barely able to raise his head from a cup of black coffee.

"What happened?"

"You wouldn't understand."

"Where have you been? We haven't seen you for days."

"I've been home—mostly."

"But what happened to you?" Arnie repeated.

His uncle rubbed his eyes with the back of his hand, then scratched his beard, thoughtfully. "I have a lady friend," he began. "She is a very nice lady. I mean **real** nice. She really is. I suppose you don't like girls yet."

"They're all right," Arnie admitted.

His uncle laughed and continued, "Anyway, I liked her a lot—almost as much as you and your mother. She makes great baked bread—homemade. When it's fresh hot, it's fantastic. I used to take her for walks. We'd go down by the river

57

and watch the tugs and barges and the lights come on in the city."

"Why didn't you bring her over here?" Arnie questioned.

"No reason. It just didn't ever work out. Well, I only met her a short time ago."

"Is she pretty?"

"Uh-huh. Well, she's no raving beauty, but she's pretty enough for me. You know I'm no great shakes myself."

Arnie laughed and looked at his uncle's crooked nose. "So what happened?" Arnie persisted.

"You remember that vision I had?" his uncle asked in reply.

"Vision?"

"The snake and the mouse."

"Oh, yeah. I remember."

"It was a portent," his uncle said.

"What's that?"

"Like a warning, like something that tells that something bad is going to happen."

"What?" Arnie asked eagerly.

For a long time his uncle considered the question, rubbing his chin. Finally he said, "Well, this girl, she was a coun-

58

try girl, born and raised on a farm over in Wisconsin. She likes farms, just like me; said she would have been happy being a farmer's wife.''

"What was her name?" Arnie asked.

"Virginia. Ain't that a pretty name?"

"Sure is."

"I think she wanted to get married, but I told her I was too old. Of course, that ain't true. I guess I was just trying to tell her that at my age I didn't want to get tied down. Anyway, we were friends and I would go over to visit her and sample her home-made bread. I liked her, too.'' His uncle smiled broadly indicating he had meant to make a joke. After a sip of coffee, he added, "She was pretty lonely. It's real tough for someone coming from the country to the city. You've lived here all your life, Arnie, so you wouldn't understand. Back home on the farm you're a part of something. People know all about you. Here you're a part of nothing. Oh, maybe a job for a while, but that's really not much.

Trying to understand, Arnie nodded. His uncle went on. "I don't mean to be mean to people 'cause I know how it hurts, but I was mean to her 'cause I told her I didn't need her. She needed me, loved me, but, well, I was just afraid. Anyway, a few days ago I went over to her place and she was gone. Her stuff was there, but she was gone. Well, I figured right away she was in the river.''

"In the river!" Arnie exclaimed.

"Yeah. I figured she couldn't take the loneliness. We talked about that one night, you know, the river, but I never believed she'd do it. Then, when she was gone like that, I figured she'd done it.''

Arnie thought, "Done it?" and thought of what that meant.

His uncle said, "Well, thank God, she didn't do it, I found out later. What happened was that one day she just up and left. Packed her clothes, took her money and went home. Didn't tell anybody—just took off. Finally she wrote a letter.'' After a pause he remarked, "Guess I could of been nicer to her. Now I really miss her.''

Each day after that Arnie thought about loneliness and what it must be like for the old lady in the gravel pit. She was all alone—except for the cats. Of course, she might be used to it by now. If no one ever came to see her, then she had no one to miss. Anyway, Arnie thought about helping her in some way. As yet he didn't quite know what to do. Perhaps he could visit her or give her a present.

On his way home from school one day, with a light shower forcing him from one store front to another, he thought of buying her a raincoat or rubbers. Perhaps a sweater. Her clothes had seemed awfully ragged and the coat she wore was always dragging on the ground.

He considered the problem for several days. It became very important to choose the right gift and more and more it began to appear: the right one was one that would make life less lonely for the old lady.

Actually it had been at the back of his mind for a long time: the only thing that would comfort her. It was a Bible! Yes, that would do it all right. Then she would have company on long lonely nights. Yes, she would certainly like that. After all, old ladies always like to read the Bible.

Chapter Five

Secret Agents

Four large sheets of white paper had been taped together to make a map of the city. The streets were sketched in wide bold lines of purple crayon. With the map laid out on the floor of Arnie's room, Arnie and Little C studied it so they could plot their next safari.

"Where we gonna explore?" asked Little C, who was really not so little, but whose older brother, Clarence, already had been nicknamed Big C.

It was their Saturday game: either exploring, spying, fighting battles or going on special secret missions. Each time, after tracing their route on the map, they went to a different section of the city. Sometimes they marked the spots of fierce battles, names of castles, fortresses and Indian camps. If they were frontier scouts like Kit Carson or Daniel Boone, they would show a trail through dense forests. City parks or areas cleared for development were usually forests. The freeways were dangerous, crocodile infested rivers. The large hotels and office buildings in the heart of the city were fortresses, castles or enormous prisons.

"See this?" Arnie pointed to a purple square.

Little C nodded. He could see that the spot under Arnie's finger was just off the freeway entrance into downtown.

"That whole block is a fortress-prison like," Arnie continued.

"Okay. So?"

"One of our secret agents is kept prisoner there. It's a huge old-fashioned fortress where they've got dungeons and stuff. We gotta get him out." Arnie squinted hard at Little C to let him know how dangerous the mission would be.

"What's his name?" Little C asked.

Arnie thought a moment, then answered, "Oh - ah - C. His name is C. It's code."

"Oh." Little C looked pleased.

"And he's got the enemy's code in his shoe so we gotta get him out—or, at least, his shoe."

Little C squinted back at Arnie.

So they took a bus to the fortress. That was part of the game, since the bus could be a helicopter, submarine, jet, ship, rocket, almost anything.

It was a beautiful day. The sky appeared free of smog and its blueness rose high above the towering blue IDS Building, the city's tallest.

"Great day," Little C remarked as he looked down Tenth Street, then up at all the castles.

"Pretend it's rainy and stormy," Arnie urged. "It's cold and wet and we're drenched 'cause we just came through a thick swamp in the middle of the night."

Little C shrugged. He was used to Arnie's wild imagination.

Inside, in the hotel lobby they encountered the imperial guard, at least forty or fifty men standing quietly in small groups conversing.

"We're disguised," Arnie whispered. "Just slip right through them."

"Let's put a bug on 'em," Little C suggested.

They pretended to plant a listening device on one man and then sat in a heavily cushioned sofa, held their hands to their ears and listened; however, they couldn't keep from giggling.

"Little C, they spotted us! They're gonna get us!" Arnie hissed and, leaping up, dashed out of the lobby and down a long corridor that led to the other end of the building. Little C scrambled after him.

Half-way down the corridor Little C came to an abrupt halt. To his right, through a door that led to an inner court he had spied a fancy swimming pool. Small trees and well-trimmed shrubs and flowers surrounded the pool.

Farther down the corridor Arnie stopped and turned back curiously. Little C beckoned.

When Arnie saw the pool, he said, "This is where the princess lives."

"The princess?"

"She's the daughter of the Emperor of China."

"Oh. Do we have to rescue her, too?" Little C asked. He was trying to be funny, but Arnie hadn't noticed.

"You wanna?" Arnie replied eagerly. The pool was empty. Little C shrugged. Where were they going to find a princess? He sure didn't care to wait around until one showed up. Anyway she might turn out to be an older woman of thirty or forty, not a princess at all.

So they left and rode the elevator up and down until one of the cleaning ladies caught them holding the door open with the button, then letting it go and banging it open with their hands.

"I'm gonna call the manager!" she screamed. "If he gets a-hold of you, he'll tan your hide."

She seemed all skin and bones and her hands were very large and mean-looking and she jabbed at Little C and startled him. Before she could get on the elevator, they pressed the button and went back to the lobby.

"Maybe we should go some other

place," Little C hinted.

"No. We'll just use the stairs," Arnie answered. "We have to find the secret agent."

"Maybe he's down in the dungeon."

Just then a tall young man with a very lean face full of pock-marks collared them.

"What are you two doing here?" he growled.

Arnie struggled against the pressure of his boney fingers.

"Just a minute, you!" the man snapped. "I seen ya foolin' around here and I'm gonna take ya to the manager." Then he began to drag Arnie and Little C toward the main desk. "I'm the assistant manager here. We don't stand for no foolin' around!"

However, before they had gone far, a man in uniform, a bell boy, who wasn't a boy but an older man with gray hair, called to them. The assistant manager stopped, turned and relaxed his grip.

The bell boy, who scarcely noticed Arnie and Little C, said, "You're supposed to go to the bank."

"Who says?" the younger man asked.

"The manager, Mr. Dieter. Who do you think?"

"Oh."

It was, apparently, such exciting news the young man dashed off without another word, leaving Arnie and Little C completely dumbfounded. In fact, Arnie was a little disappointed since he had viewed the trip to the manager's office as another part of their adventure; it would have been a trip to the torture chamber.

The bell boy asked, "What was that all about?"

Automatically Little C shrugged a reply, but Arnie blurted, "He was taking us to see the manager."

"What were you doing?"

"Nothin'. Just goofin' around."

"Yeah, he thinks he's pretty important," the man commented, smiled and, after a moment, added, "Go play. Behave yourselves though." As they eased away, he whispered, "Stay out of the grouch's way."

After that, following Little C's suggestion, they went down into the dungeon, followed cold, dark passageways dripping with moisture and filled with screeching vampires, cob webs and eery drafts that swirled around them. Arnie struck an imaginary match to light his imaginary candle and led them deep into the fort-ress-prison. On the way they came to a place where the basement housed two shops, a barber shop and a dry cleaners. When Arnie passed the dry cleaners and heard the hiss of the steam irons, he tackled Little C and together they sprawled onto the floor.

"A bomb went off!" he shouted. "We blasted him out."

Little C looked up to see a man looking at them through a window in the shop. The man began to laugh.

"Hey, Arnie!" Little C protested. "Get off me!"

"We gotta act fast," Arnie ordered. "You go in and get the agent out of his cell before the guards come." Then, when Arnie saw the man laughing at them, he shouted, "A guard! Run!" Scrambling to his feet, he dashed down the hallway and around the corner.

Little C shrugged at the man, raised an eyebrow as if to say, "Some people!" and then shuffled out of sight around the corner. He looked for Arnie in the hallway, but it was empty. He wondered how he could have gotten all the way to the end and around the next corner so fast. Undoubtedly Arnie would say he had been captured and thrown into a cell. Little C could just hear him. Just then Arnie bounded from a janitor's closet, grabbed Little C, pulled him inside and slammed the door shut.

"The guards are making the rounds," Arnie warned.

Inside it was pitch dark. Though he had no idea of the size of the room, Little C felt as if he were inside a little box. He stood perfectly still, not knowing where Arnie was or what objects were around him.

"Let's get out of here," Little C suggested, trying not to sound afraid.

"Wait 'til the guards go by."

"There aren't any guards." Little C was tired of the game.

"Listen!"

Together they listened to the clack of heels on the concrete floor. Little C felt his heart flutter. Arnie touched him and he almost jumped—except that he dared not move against the black walls which surrounded him. Then the sound faded. The guards had gone and once again, after a very close call, they had escaped detection. Arnie blew a sigh past Little C.

Little C's voice probed for Arnie. "Hey, Arnie, let's go, huh? Let's take the bus back. Let's pretend it's a space ship."

"We haven't found the secret agent yet," Arnie said with undiminished enthusiasm.

Reluctantly Little C followed Arnie back to the lobby so they could continue their mission. They passed the front desk casually and then, when the clerk was busy, went up a flight of stairs to a skyway and crossed over the street to a parking ramp.

Little C asked, "Where are we going now?"

"Around and around." Arnie pushed open the heavy door to the ramp, which was filled with foul exhaust odors.

"What?"

"Down the ramp, the way the cars go, around and around."

And he was about to run when Little C exclaimed, "Hey, what's that?"

Beside the door was a canvas bag. Little C stood over it — staring down. Arnie pounced on it. It looked important and official and bulging with contents. He held it out for both of them to examine. On it was the stenciled name of the hotel.

"Unzip it," Little C urged.

The padlock was not closed so Arnie opened the bag.

Little C gasped, "It's full of money!"

"Of course," Arnie said. "That's the money another secret agent left."

"Why?"

"To pay the one who's in the dungeon for the secret code."

"Oh." Little C gave a shrug. "Listen, Arnie, this is real -----."

"Our agent is supposed to pick up the money and leave the code."

Little C was getting exasperated. "Arnie, this is real money!"

"I know it."

"We ought to do something with it."

Arnie suggested, "Let's spend it." Then he looked into the bag so Little C

couldn't see his expression.

Little C looked into the bag also. "Gee! There must be a million dollars here."

"We could sure buy a lot with that," Arnie said.

"Gee, Arnie!" Little C looked frightened. "Gosh! I couldn't bring anything home, anything big. My Mom and Dad would - - - - - -."

Arnie's laughter interrupted Little C, whose mouth dropped. "I was just kidding," said Arnie. "What d'ya think I am, a crook? Sure we gotta do something. We gotta take it back."

An idea lit Little C's face. "Maybe there's a reward!"

Arnie agreed. "It must of come from the hotel safe," said Arnie. Then: "Yeah! Remember that mean guy who grabbed us? He was going to the bank."

"He dropped it or something."

"Maybe he hid it."

"Yeah! He was mean."

"Maybe he's a crook."

"We gotta take this right back to the manager," Arnie exclaimed.

"Right on!" echoed Little C.

They started to zip up the bag, but then had trouble when a crisp bill became caught in the zipper. At that moment a car came around the circular ramp and screeched to a halt beside them. Little C looked up first. By the time Arnie turned his head, the man was out of the car and marching at them. Little C let go of the bag and backed off. Left with the money sack, which was obviously what the man was after, Arnie thought of running. Behind him was the door to the skyway, in front of him was the ramp; however, the man moved quickly to a point where he could easily cut off Arnie either way. Then Arnie looked again at the man and when he recognized the assistant manager, he almost dropped the bag.

"I got you!" the man shouted. "What are you doing with that money?"

"We were gonna take it to the manager," Little C protested from a safe distance down the ramp.

The man only shifted his eyes slightly in response to Little C. He glared at Arnie. "You give it here! That money's gotta go to the bank."

"We found it by the door," Arnie commented.

"You little crooks!" the man screamed and his scream was accidently timed with the squeal of tires from the street below.

"We're not crooks! You are!" Arnie challenged and then wondered if he should have been so brave.

"What! Why you little -------!" The man advanced and Arnie, by instinct, tossed the bag down to Little C. Then the man spun around and nearly twisted his ankle. "Give that here!" he demanded. When he advanced, Little C underhanded the sack back to Arnie.

"We weren't stealing it. We were taking it to the manager," Arnie insisted. "Why don't you let us go back so we can give it to him?"

"No! You give it to me!"

"Maybe he was stealing it," Little C suggested.

"I was taking it to the bank," the man answered.

"How come it was by the door?" Little C questioned.

"I dropped it by accident."

Holding the bag as if to toss it, Arnie

shouted, "Little C, here, take the bag and run down the ramp and go over to the hotel."

Little C was amazed. The man would surely catch him.

The man blared, "You crazy kids!"

"Here!" Arnie started swinging the bag. The assistant manager's expression suddenly changed. The anger disappeared. His shoulders drooped and his face twisted into a pained, sad expression. He looked suddenly sick.

"C'mon, you guys!" he pleaded. "I gotta get that money to the bank or I'll lose my job. I'm not stealing it or anything. I put it on the roof of my car 'cause I had my hands full of packages and I was trying to unlock the car and then I forgot it and it must have slid off when I drove away. C'mon! You can come with me to the bank. I'll buy you something to eat. C'mon! I'm sorry I was mean. Whatever you do, don't go to the manager. He'll fire me sure as blazes."

"How much money is it?" Arnie asked.

"About five thousand," the man answered. Arnie and the man stared at each

other, each sizing up the other. Finally
the man said, "I can't give you a reward.
I only got a couple dollars on me, but you
can have that. Please, huh?"

Because of the change in his manner,
Arnie decided to trust him and held out
the bag.

"Thanks," the man said. He took the
bag and placed it in the crook of his arm.
Then he reached into his back pocket for
his billfold. "I appreciate this, you
guys, especially after I was kind of tough
on you." He extracted two dollars from
his billfold.

"That's okay," Arnie said and backed
away from the money.

"Take it." The man offered it again.

But Arnie was equally persistent. "No.
It's all right."

Then the man smiled. "You're sure?"
Arnie nodded. For the first time the
man's face did not seem mean-looking.
"Thanks a lot," he said. He returned to
his car and drove down the ramp.

After they could hear his car no longer,
Little C said with a sigh, "Well! How
about that?"

"Yeah," Arnie answered. "Let's go."

"Where?"

"We gotta go back and get that secret code."

With a shrug Little C followed as Arnie led the way back to the prison-fortress.

Chapter Six

The Fishing Trip

Arnie's father and mother separated before Arnie was old enough to know what was happening. All he knew was that his father only came to the house afterwards as a visitor. And gradually he learned that that would always be the way he saw his father.

As he grew older and understood more, he sometimes wondered about the reasons why it had happened. Basically it was a mystery to him. Oh, he knew that grown-ups did these things, but he still worried about the cause of it. Perhaps he was afraid to know. That was why he didn't ask questions.

One day Gop happened to offer Arnie a clue about his father. They had been talking about what Arnie would do when he grew up. "I hope you're not restless like your dad," Gop had said. "Now there was a man who couldn't be tied down. Always on the go—doing this, doing that!"

At other times he heard snatches of conversations between Gop and his mother or between his uncle and his mother, but he never put all the pieces of the puzzle together.

What bothered Arnie most was not having both parents come to the school at open house or other times like that. Sometimes he made up excuses for his father's absence. There were times, too, when he would have liked to have had his father around to take him to a ball-game or fishing. Of course, his uncle did that a lot, but it was not the same. And his mother worked so she didn't have time. Besides, what did a woman know about fishing?

Therefore, it surprised Arnie one day when his mother asked him if he wanted to go on a fishing trip. "Well, do you?" she repeated when he looked dumbfounded.

"Sounds great," he said, uncertainly.

She had come in in a flurry, carrying a large blue paper bag from one of the department stores.

"What's that?" he asked.

"Well, if we're going fishing, we have to have new outfits."

She pulled a sundress and a jacket out of the bag. "Isn't that nice?" Then she held up two pieces of a bathing suit, a floppy hat, sunglasses the size of two saucers and finally a pair of sandals. "Here's something for you, Arnie!" She gave him a blue T-shirt with a leaping swordfish across the front. "And this!" Her face was beaming. It was a pair of blue Adidas. "Now wait!" she squealed, ran back into the hall and returned with a long narrow box. Right away Arnie guessed it was fishing gear.

"Hey! Gee!" He leaped at it. He'd never expected that!

Then his mother said in that funny way adults have when they want approval from children, "A friend of your moth-

er's. . . . .asked us. . . . .to go. . . . .
a very nice man.''

She watched him intently. Though he
looked down at his things, he could feel
her gaze. When he looked up, she was
holding the sundress in front of her. It
appeared just the right size. He didn't
know what to say. Finally she smiled
and sent him into his room to try on his
clothes. Later she informed him the man
would pick them up in the afternoon.

Arnie stayed in his room thinking
about the man and wondered what this
fishing trip would mean. Once his
mother came in and stuttered through a
speech about the man. His name was
George Redman and he was ''a very nice
man''. She repeated that several times.
It bothered Arnie to see her working so
hard to please him.

When George Redman finally came,
Arnie closed the door to his room. He
listened to their voices. Their laughter
disturbed him. Then the door opened
and his mother came in. He noticed the
burst of excitement in her face. She
looked attractive in the new sundress, a
bright grass-green with a light cotton

jacket to match.

"Arnie. . . . ." she began hesitantly,
then turned and George Redman stepped
out from behind her.

He was not as tall or muscular as
Arnie's father. His hair was flecked with
gray and he wore glasses. He smiled
hopefully. He extended his hand and
Arnie shook it, but only because he had
to.

Arnie's mother began talking about the
trip, speaking rapidly, nervously. Even-
tually she pointed out Arnie's new
fishing rod.

George Redman nodded, smiled, then
picked it up from the bed. "I'll fix it up
for you, Arnie," he said in a high-pitched,
almost timid voice.

*   *   *

They drove north into the lake country.
Redman had a camper in a pick-up truck
and Arnie lay in the sleeper above the
cab. Though the whine of the wheels,
the rush of the wind along the sides and
the creak of metal were constant sounds,
Arnie also heard laughter from below
him and he felt lonely and rejected.

In spite of that, he was thrilled by the sights: the lush green land stretching out like a carpet, the fast moving streams, the water alive with silver swimming ripples, the irregular interruptions of meadows and woods, a sky of such solid blue it seemed to have been painted with enamel.

He lay on his stomach, his face pressed to the window and followed the progress of the blue hood of the pick-up as it steadily, evenly devoured the blacktop.

Later, at night, with the headlights beaming ahead, they drove down a narrow lane with tree branches screeching against the side of the camper. Then, when they entered a clearing, Arnie could see the flat expanse of water. Lights flicked off the surface, reminding him of the submerged lights of a swimming pool. Though his view was limited, the sense of the lake excited him. It was out there groaning behind the darknss, lapping at the land like some gigantic cat.

The cabin consisted of two small bedrooms, a bath and a large room with stove, refrigerator, cupboard, kitchen table and chairs, a sofa and two easy chairs. The walls were paneled with plain pine board containing a strong wood smell, the windows hung with green paper curtains.

Arnie's mother bounced on one of the beds, testing it. "Wow! Aren't these nice!" she joked.

Redman laughed. "Just like the Hilton." He dropped the luggage inside the door.

Arnie was eyeing George Redman distrustfully when he turned and addressed him. "Well, do you want the sleeping bag or should I take it? We'd better give your mother one of the beds."

Arnie took the sleeping bag. Later in the darkness he wondered why it couldn't be just the two of them—he and his mother. Why did this stranger have to intrude where he wasn't wanted?

*   *   *

Early the next morning Redman shook Arnie and whispered, "Let's go get some fish for breakfast."

For a moment Arnie could remember

nothing. Where was he? Whose face was bending over him? Then he saw his mother's head resting on a pillow in the bedroom, her long blonde hair laid out around her head like a doily. Looking up at the bare rafters, he saw a naked bulb attached to a two-by-four.

Redman said, "Arnie, wake up. You said you'd go fishing with me this morning."

Arnie dragged himself out of the sleeping bag. With his first glimpse of the lake he thought it the color of aluminum. Above, the sky was covered with ugly gray clouds. A chill breeze cut through his light windbreaker. It was a terrible morning and he felt sick because of it.

"This is cold north country," Redman shouted from the camper.

Arnie ran to the dock. There the water looked a murky gray-green, with occasional streaks of blue. While he stood there a school of minnows swam by. Out from the dock a spout of water suddenly erupted and he knew it was a fish. He felt the excitement growing inside of him.

The wind picked up. Arnie shivered. The lake looked cold. Redman came to him with a leather fur-lined jacket. "Here, Arnie, put this on. That's an old-time flight jacket."

Redman knelt on the dock, readying the fishing gear. "Look at the white caps, Arnie."

Arnie did not have to be told what white caps were. The water everywhere was scooped with white foam. The waves slapped resoundingly on the beach. He thought of the ocean and a violent storm; however, Redman did not show any signs of worry. When they launched the aluminum fishing boat into the wind, a cold spray showered them. Arnie felt like crawling down in the boat.

Because of the noise of the motor and the hard dull slap of the boat against the waves, they didn't talk until they came to a protected bay. There the wind passed overhead and the sound seemed distant. On a ridge they could see the trees arching toward them.

After Redman anchored, he showed Arnie how to cast with his new spinning reel. "The owner of the resort said this is a good spot so we'll just sit here and cast for a while," Redman remarked.

In time Arnie caught on to casting. Then it was fun. He kept one eye on Redman and tried to work the lure as he did. After it was going easy, Redman began to chat. Arnie was surprised when he spoke so openly about himself.

He was divorced. "Just like your mother," he said, but the word shocked Arnie. It sounded like some horrible disease. He had two daughters, whom he did not see very often, was an electrical contractor and lived on a small farm where he raised horses and a few cattle as a hobby. As it happened, he traveled in his work just as Arnie's father did, often to western states.

"You should see some of that country" he said, referring to the mountains of Colorado and Idaho.

His descriptions were vivid. Arnie was looking off across the water, picturing the mountains when something happened which completely startled him. His rod jerked violently, almost springing from his hand and the line screeched, running out.

Arnie screamed, panic-stricken, "What do I do?"

Redman's voice was calm. "Keep your hand on the crank, but let him have it. Keep the pressure on. Not too much. Don't jerk it. That's it. Hold the rod up." He brought one hand around and started turning the handle for Arnie. "Like this." Then he sat back and let Arnie do it.

Arnie's heart was thumping. The rod bent down and the tip almost touched the water.

"Atta boy, Arnie!" Redman shouted encouragingly.

Arnie was drawing the fish slowly toward the boat, turning the reel one precious crank at a time. Occasionally it would whirr as the fish shook and ran away. His rod was tipped under water now. All of a sudden he saw a dark object scoot for cover under the boat.

"It's a fish!" he cried.

Redman laughed. "What did you expect?" Then: "Must be a good-sized Northern. Hold your rod away from the boat."

The rod wanted to fly out of Arnie's hand. He fought the fish, tugging, then getting a response from the other end.

"I can't hold it!" He could no longer turn the handle, his arms and hands ached and he was sure that if the fish gave another good jerk, he would lose it.

"Hang on, Arnie!"

"I can't."

"Yes, you can."

"No! No!"

Just then the fish did a crazy pirouette beneath them.

"Give him just a little line," Redman ordered.

"What's he doing?"

"Steady. Pull up a little with the rod."

Arnie started to stand and he felt the boat slipping out from under him. Again the fish twirled and Arnie could feel the movement in the rod. Then it bent in half, nearly pulling him out of the boat. At that moment Redman's arm hooked around him and pulled him down.

"Take it easy! You almost went overboard."

It was all exciting, especially when he realized he had almost fallen in. He felt Redman's hand on his waist.

"This bugger is really tough!" he bellowed, glancing at Redman, who nodded.

Now Arnie was determined to land it. He managed to reel in a little more line. The fish was immediately below him and when he saw it balancing there, he called, "Holy Cow! He's a monster!"

As it began to surface, Redman dug under it with a net and, with some difficulty, hoisted it into the boat where it thrashed and whacked against their gear. It was a Northern, about fifteen pounds. It still seemed ferocious. Arnie stared in amazement at the gaudy mouth, the jagged teeth. He sat back and let himself go, trembling. His muscles were jumping from the constant tension.

They tried fishing some more, but Arnie was so eager to show his catch to his mother, they pulled anchor and motored back. She was waiting on the dock. Arnie could scarcely lift the fish, which was nearly as long as he.

She was delighted. "Wonderful! Oh, I'm so happy, Arnie! That's a fantastic fish!"

Redman agreed. "You don't see many like that."

In an undertone she confessed to Redman, "It's ugly. My goodness! It looks dangerous.''

Arnie thought they would eat it, but Redman suggested it be stuffed and took it off to the owner of the resort. Because it was Redman's idea, Arnie didn't like it at all.

"It's to eat," he complained to his mother.

"He wants to do that for you. Now let him!'' his mother scolded.

Arnie didn't say any more, but he thought, It isn't fair! Why should she take his side? And he believed the two of them were against him.

The day continued overcast, the wind cold. They sat in the cabin and played cards. Redman couldn't understand Arnie's moodiness after catching the great fish. Soon Arnie tired of playing and went into a corner and read. His mother was embarrassed by his behavior. Later she and Redman went to get groceries.

Alone, Arnie brooded. He compared Redman with his father and then became upset because he thought Redman wanted to take his father's place. That was why he was so pleasant and laughed and joked and always called him "Arnie" with such special emphasis.

Toward evening the cap of clouds blew away, the wind died and the sun showed low in the western sky. The water changed to blue. Arnie went for a walk along the beach. From time to time he thought about the experience with the fish. Then he heard the whirr of the reel, saw the fish diving and felt the thrill all over. If only it had been his father there instead of Redman!

After a while Arnie stopped and played in the sand. He cupped out holes, plowed trenches and then filled them with water. Engrossed, he did not notice a silver hull moving directly at him. The sound of the motor was scarcely heard above the smack of the waves on the beach. Soon, however, it crunched into the lake bottom near him. It was Redman and his mother.

Redman's face was burned and his freckles stood out, making him appear boyish, even less like Arnie's father. He said, "We're going back and get another one like this morning," and beckoned to Arnie.

After they were underway, Redman

offered Arnie the motor. "It's okay," he assured him. "Just keep the bow in line with that cabin." He indicated a dwelling on a distant point. Then he showed Arnie the throttle and how to steer. Though he resented Redman as much as ever, Arnie was thrilled.

Redman called over his shoulder, "I hope you get another one just like this morning."

As luck would have it, they didn't. They did, however, catch a good mess of pan fish and it was almost as much fun. Both Arnie and Redman laughed with delight when Arnie's mother squealed catching a little sunfish. Redman helped her take it off the hook. It was more fun watching her than anything, Arnie thought.

That night they fried and ate their catch. "There's nothing better than fish right out of the lake," Redman declared.

It was pleasant with the stars and moon out. The moon was in the southeast, low in the sky. For a while they sat on the dock and watched the sky and lake blend.

Arnie asked Redman why they didn't

sleep in the camper.

"You can if you want to," he answered. "It's just that I don't have the stove or refrigerator hooked up and I thought we'd be more comfortable in the cabin."

Then Arnie's mother said, "Arnie, that would be fun for you. Why don't you?"

But Arnie was reluctant. Actually he would have loved it, but he still felt that jealousy and didn't want them to be alone.

His mother said, "Well, we'd like to sit up for a while. Why don't you sleep in one of the bedrooms and later we'll move you back to where you slept last night?"

They went inside and Arnie got into his mother's bed. He felt cheated. Instead of sleeping he made all sorts of noises, forcing his mother to look in on him. He told her he was having a nightmare. Then he tossed and turned and set the bed springs to twanging. He called for water and aspirin. "I think I'm going to throw up," he said.

She felt his forehead. "You don't feel warm."

After she was gone only a short time, he opened the door. It was too warm. Redman came in and opened the window. Then it was too cold. When that was remedied, he definitely had to vomit. Though he didn't, he went back and forth to the bathroom several times. Finally they gave up and went to bed.

Arnie decided he had won a victory. He curled up inside the sleeping bag, planning to dream of the fish; however, instead he had bad dreams about his mother, father and Redman. In the morning he could not remember the details, but he suffered from an uneasy feeling.

Before breakfast the three of them went swimming. Arnie splashed his mother and had a great time diving off the floating raft anchored out from shore. Redman was an expert diver and showed them a variety of dives. All that served, however, was to cause further irritation for Arnie.

In the water his mother seemed graceful and Arnie hunched down so that only his head was above the water and studied her. In that way he felt concealed from Redman, who was cavorting and showing off. He dived under water acting like a marauding shark searching for Arnie's mother's legs. She screeched and thrashed about trying to escape. Arnie stayed back, disgusted with this display.

He thought Redman looked ugly without his glasses and with his hair plastered down.

Then suddenly the two of them were playing and splashing water and excluding Arnie. Their laughter attacked him. His mother turned her back, moving away from him, pulling at the water with cupped hands. She was running from Redman. A few moments later she was shouting, laughing, crying, attempting to protect herself from the cascade of water Redman had set up. Furious, Arnie cut a path to Redman and started beating him on the chest.

"Leave my mother alone!" he sobbed. He landed a number of punches before Redman clutched him by the wrists.

"Arnie!" his mother wailed, horrified. "Arnie! Arnie!"

"It's all right," Redman assured her,

though he seemed astounded. "Okay, Arnie, Okay." And he released him.

Arnie understood enough to be intensely embarrassed and, without a glance at either of them, ran off to the woods behind the resort. The tall pines provided a shelter so he ran into the center of the grove. He sat down and waited for them to come for him. He thought of their cruelty, torturing him as they had, making him feel not wanted. He thought of his own stupidity. How could he ever face them again! He hated Redman!

From a distance he heard his mother's voice. He did not answer. The long silence which followed led him to suspect they were circling him. Several times he thought he heard the crunch of pine cones, but a quick survey revealed nothing. Maybe they would give up and leave him.

Finally, without any warning he saw Redman's legs. He was facing Arnie, evidently peering into the trees. Arnie held perfectly still. Let them come in to get him!

While concentrating on Redman, he

had forgotten his mother. He should have known they would be acting together. Why did it have to be the two of them against him? Again he felt betrayed. At any rate, his mother caught him by surprise. By the sound of her voice he knew she had spotted him.

Spinning around, he saw her advancing stooped over. "Arnie! Now come out!" Obviously she had reached the end of her patience. "We're going and we don't have time ------!"

All right! He surrendered, slinking out, ducking down to run our from under her hand. He ran to the cabin. There he waited for the scolding from his mother; however, it never came. Instead she and Redman turned away from him and, speechlessly, went about packing.

His mother's hands-off policy was worse than if she had spanked him. From then on she acted as if he were something contagious. While they packed, he sat moping by the pick-up.

On the way back it was much quieter. He heard no laughter from below. Recalling their glances while packing and loading, Arnie became convinced something had gone wrong between them. His mother's eyes, for example, seemed to contain as much hostility for Redman as for him.

Several days later when Arnie's uncle asked them about the trip, his mother passed over it quickly. Her swift glance at Arnie went unnoticed by his uncle. Soon the trip was forgotten. It disappointed Arnie that they didn't get to talk about his fish, but, considering his mother's looks, he didn't dare bring it up. Even when alone with his uncle or his friends, he didn't mention it. It was as if the weekend had never occurred.

One day about two weeks later Arnie's mother asked him about the fish. "Do you want the fish?"

"What?"

"The fish. The fish you caught. Do you want it? It's stuffed."

Reflecting, he turned to look into his room. Where would he put it? Already the walls were filled with pictures and posters. He studied his mother while she busied herself at the sink. What would she want? Would she want to have it in the house? Wouldn't it just be a reminder of a bad time?

As if guessing his thoughts, she advised, "You do what you want. It's up to you."

"Okay," he said, but did not give her an answer. He went into his room to think about it.

Then one day his mother said to him, "Mr. Redman's bringing the fish over tomorrow so you'd better decide what to do."

That night after supper he went in search of his uncle. He wanted to know what she had told him about Redman. Did she like him? Would they, someday, get married? His uncle did not know. She had not talked to him at all.

His uncle asked, "What happened on that fishing trip? Ever since, your mother's been going around with a chip on her shoulder. I get the feeling that if I say anything, she'll bite my head off."

Arnie said nothing had happened, that it was just an ordinary fishing trip. However, after a few moments he asked, "Do you think Mom likes Redman?"

His uncle shrugged. "I'd say she liked him if she brought him home to get her family's approval.''

"Her 'family'?'' Arnie asked, perplexed.

"You! You're her family.''

"Oh. Oh! Me?'' That's a small family, he thought. Still a family's a family. So she brought him for that! Gee, I didn't give him a chance!

Then in a rush, because he felt so ashamed, he confessed how he'd been mean to his mother and Redman and had spoiled their weekend and, worse, had made it so Redman didn't want to see his mother anymore and now had ruined his mother's life.

"What should I do?'' Arnie pleaded, finally.

"I dunno,'' his uncle replied. "Anyway, you should apologize. Start with that. Say you were sorry.''

The next night, because he was expecting Redman, Arnie was nervous. He was home in plenty of time since he wanted to think about what to say, first to his mother and then to Redman. He had to let them know that he would never stand between them again or try to make them unhappy.

Soon he heard his mother's footsteps, looked at the clock and realized he had wasted his time and had not thought of what to say. For a second he thought of hiding in his room, but hesitated and then she was at the door, pulling it open, catching him standing in the kitchen. She was carrying the fish. Though it was wrapped loosely in manilla wrapping paper, he recognized it. His fish! The tail was protruding. His mother struggled with the awkward, bulky form.

"Here's your fish!" she groaned, hitching it up on her hip, lugging it to the table. "What a dumb idea! What are we going to do with this hideous thing?" She ripped off the paper. "Look at it!" she exclaimed. "Isn't it awful?" It appeared as it had when it floundered in the bottom of the boat, ferocious and mean, but helpless.

Mounted on a board, its body frozen in an arch, the mouth open wide, the fish was only a poor reminder of that fighting fish. It had a waxy, unreal look.

Arnie asked, "Where did you get it?"

"From George Redman."

"I thought he was going to bring it."

"No. He dropped it off at work today." She crumpled the paper and tossed it in the basket, came back to the table, looked down at the fish and sighed. "I hate to have that thing in this house."

Arnie felt sorry for Redman. "He was just trying to be nice."

"You didn't think that at the time," she said.

"I know, but I do now. I was wrong. I'm sorry about how I acted."

"I'm glad," she replied.

"Aren't you seeing him anymore?" Arnie asked.

"I see him now and then. We're still friends." Then she looked at Arnie, reddening. He hadn't wanted to cause her any embarrassment. It was this business, difficult for adults, of having to explain something they didn't want to to children. Finally she blurted, "Just forget about the whole thing. Okay? Go do something in your room."

Ignoring this, he said, "You can see Mr. Redman. It's all right with me. And if you want to marry ------."

"Thanks a lot," she said, trying to

smile.

"No! Really! I'm sorry for acting the way I did."

"Good."

"You can do whatever you want. I'll never act that way again."

"That's good to hear." She turned and went to the sink where she began to prepare their meal. Arnie stood nearby expecting to hear more on the subject, but she went about her work as if she did not know he was there. Arnie grew impatient.

She was about to peel potatoes when he asked, "Did you and Mr. Redman break-up?"

"I guess so," she responded quietly, then turned on the water, which splashed noisely into a pan.

"It's all my fault!" he cried.

"Because you acted like a little kid on that fishing trip?" she asked without turning. She began cutting the potatoes into the pan.

"Yeah. He couldn't stand me," Arnie muttered.

"Well, he would have had to learn to stand you if he was going to marry me because we're a package deal," she said. Then with a faint smile she moved from the sink to the stove. "But that wasn't it. As bad as you were, that wasn't it, so don't worry. And I won't worry either now that I know you'll let me lead my own life. If I want to marry someone, I'll just do it, huh? I won't have to ask your permission?"

Arnie nodded and afterwards his mother came to him and hugged him and laughed pleasantly. "Okay," she said. "Go hang up your smelly old fish."